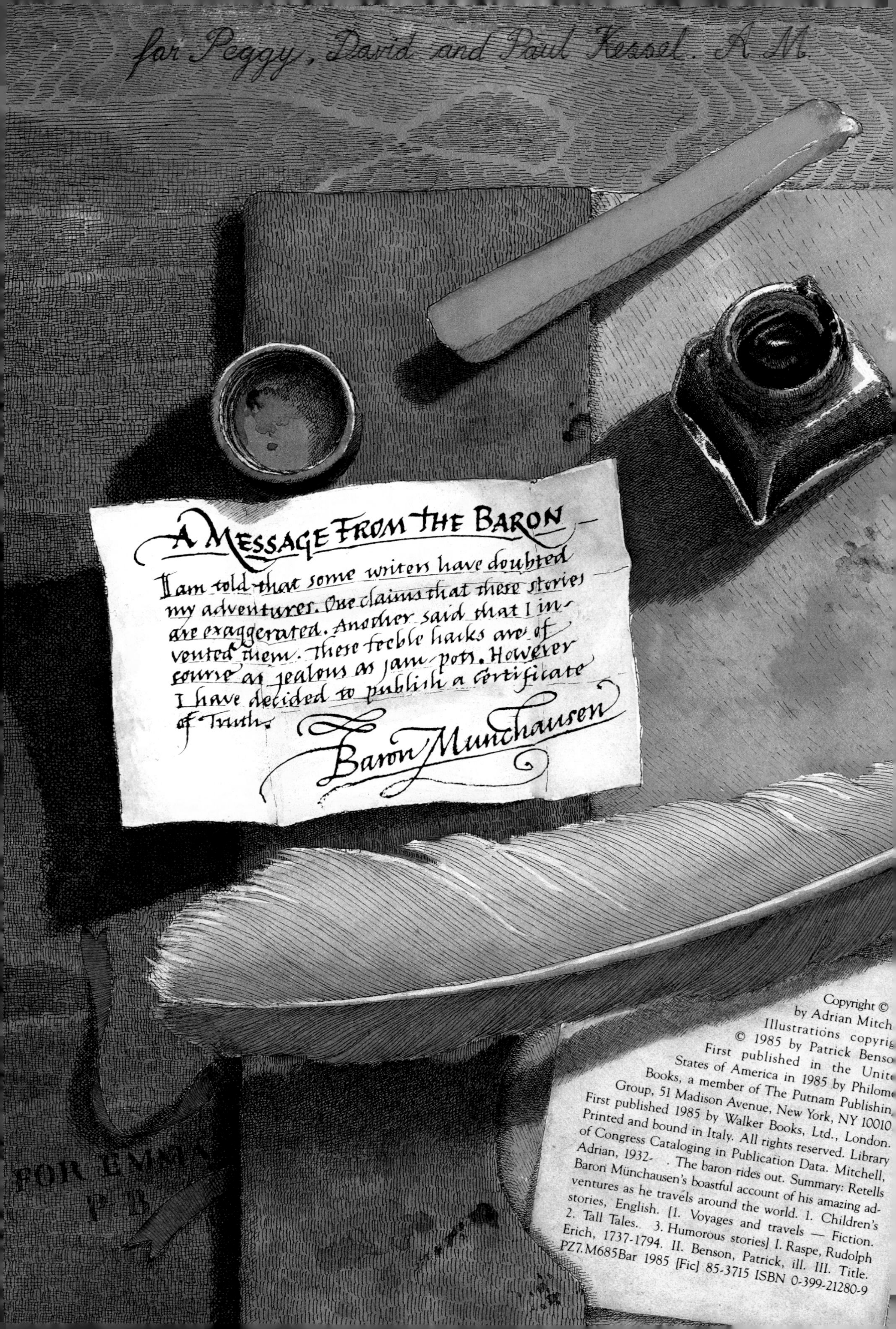

First published in the Unite
States of America in 1985 by Philome
Books, a member of The Putnam Publishin
Group, 51 Madison Avenue, New York, NY 10010.
First published 1985 by Walker Books, Ltd., London.
Printed and bound in Italy. Library
of Congress Cataloging in Publication Data. Mitchell,
Adrian, 1932- . The baron rides out. Summary: Retells
Baron Münchausen's boastful account of his amazing ad-
ventures as he travels around the world. 1. Children's
stories, English. [1. Voyages and travels — Fiction.
2. Tall Tales. 3. Humorous stories] I. Raspe, Rudolph
Erich, 1737-1794. II. Benson, Patrick, ill. III. Title.
PZ7.M685Bar 1985 [Fic] 85-3715 ISBN 0-399-21280-9

CERTIFICATE OF TRUTH
We the undersigned do swear that
the adventures of Baron Munchausen
in whatever country they may be
are all as true as tricycles
Aladdin
Captain Sinbad
Pinocchio.
Lemuel Gulliver
The Baron Rides Out
The Adventures of
BARON MUNCHAUSEN
as he told them
to
ADRIAN MITCHELL
With pictures
drawn on horseback
by
PATRICK BENSON
Philomel Books
New York
M

I was less than a man but more than a boy when I decided to leave home and see the world.

My father shouted, my mother swore and my 48 younger brothers and sisters begged me to stay. But I was as firm as a fortress.

"If you must go, you must go," said my parents. They often said the same thing at the same time.

My 48 younger brothers and sisters used their pocket money to buy me a farewell present. They gave me a large parcel. I unwrapped it on the lawn.

Out stepped a fine horse. "But it's wild!" shouted my mother and father, "wild as a windmill!"

For the horse was standing on its hind legs. It gnashed its teeth and lashed out with its front hooves. It chased my parents and my 48 brothers and sisters three times around our castle (about 33 miles).

Then it came up to me, rolling its crazy eyes. I returned its stare. Then I somersaulted onto its back, grabbed its mane and whispered three words into its left ear.

The brute calmed down at once. My parents and brothers and sisters had retired to the tea-room upstairs.

Luckily the window was open, so I urged my horse to jump through it. The beast landed delicately in the middle of the tea-table.

There he walked, trotted, cantered and galloped without breaking one cup or saucer. My family were delighted with this performance.

"Please leave home now and see the world," said my dear mother and father as one parent. With a wave and a leap my horse and I were on the lawn. Within seconds we had disappeared over the horizon. And that's as true as trumpeters.

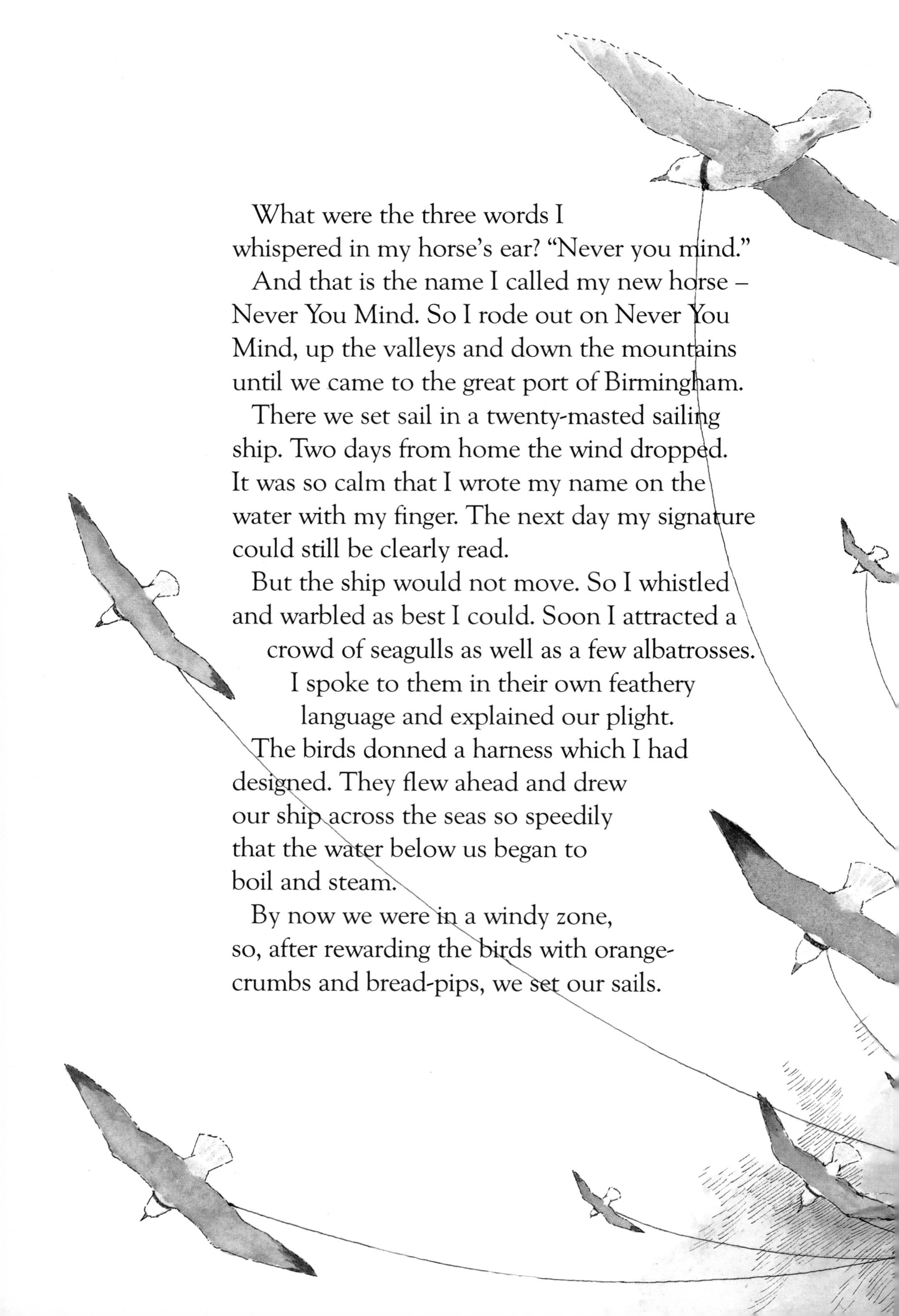

What were the three words I whispered in my horse's ear? "Never you mind."

And that is the name I called my new horse – Never You Mind. So I rode out on Never You Mind, up the valleys and down the mountains until we came to the great port of Birmingham.

There we set sail in a twenty-masted sailing ship. Two days from home the wind dropped. It was so calm that I wrote my name on the water with my finger. The next day my signature could still be clearly read.

But the ship would not move. So I whistled and warbled as best I could. Soon I attracted a crowd of seagulls as well as a few albatrosses. I spoke to them in their own feathery language and explained our plight.

The birds donned a harness which I had designed. They flew ahead and drew our ship across the seas so speedily that the water below us began to boil and steam.

By now we were in a windy zone, so, after rewarding the birds with orange-crumbs and bread-pips, we set our sails.

Soon we dropped anchor at the island of Ceylon. We took on board wood, water and toffee. It was a humdrum visit, except for the storm.

A mighty wind tore up the island's trees by the roots. Some of them weighed many tons. But the wind carried them so high that, from the ground, they looked like the feathers of little birds.

At dawn the storm stopped suddenly. All the trees fell about five miles straight downwards into their proper places and took root again. All except one.

This was the largest tree of all. When it was blown up into the air a man and a woman, a very honest old couple, were gathering cucumbers on its branches.

As the tree fell, their weight overbalanced it. It landed on the King of the island, who was killed at once.

He had left his house to go shopping for a new crown when this lucky accident happened. I say lucky, for the King was a very greedy and cruel man. All his subjects were as happy as hippos to see him squashed.

They chose the old cucumber couple to rule over them and built them a yellow seven-storey palace made entirely from banana skins.

And that's as true as tragedy.

As for me, I rode off into the interior of Ceylon upon Never You Mind. As we paused at a river to drink, I thought I heard a rustling noise. Turning round I was interested to see an enormous lion.

He was striding towards me. His tongue lolled from his mouth. It was obvious that he wanted to eat me for lunch and have Never You Mind for dessert.

What was to be done? My rifle was only loaded with swan-shot. This would kill nothing bigger than a small wombat.

I am well-known as a lover of animals. I decided to frighten the lion. I fired into the air. But the bang only angered him. He ran towards me at full speed.

I tried to run away. But the moment I turned from the lion I found myself face to face with a large crocodile.

Its mouth was open wide. I could have walked inside without bending my head.

So, the crocodile was in front of me. The lion was behind me. On my left was a foaming river. On my right was a precipice. At the bottom of the precipice I could see a nest of green and yellow snakes.

I gave myself up for lost. The lion rose up onto his back legs. He was ready to pounce. At that second I tripped and fell to the ground. So the lion sprang over me.

For a long moment I lay still. I expected to feel the claws of the lion in my hair and the jaws of the crocodile around my heels. Then there was an awful noise. I sat up and looked around.

Imagine my joy when I saw that the lion had jumped so far that he had jammed his head into the open mouth of the crocodile. They were struggling together, each of them trying to escape.

I drew my sword and cut off the lion's head with one stroke. Then, with the butt of my rifle, I drove the lion's head down the crocodile's throat. The crocodile died of suffocation – a brief, merciful death, I am pleased to say.

Some absurd versions of this story have been spread. In one of these, the lion jumps right down the crocodile's throat and is emerging at the other end when I cut off his head. This, of course, is impossible. I think it shameful that the truth should be treated so lightly.

I looked about me for my trusty steed, but could spy no trace of Never You Mind. Finally I found him cowering in a rabbit hole.

My timid horse had sweated with fear. He had sweated away so much of himself that he was by now no bigger than a badger.

I am a great lover of animals, and fed him upon cream buns and fried potatoes. By the time we reached Poland, one month later, I had built him up to his usual size.

Riding through the endless snows, I saw a poor beggar lying by the wayside, shivering in his rags. Although cold myself, I threw my velvet cloak over him.

At once I heard a voice from the heavens saying: "My son, you will be rewarded for this noble act."

I rode on. Darkness fell. No village was to be seen. Snow was everywhere.

Tired out, I dismounted. I tied Never You Mind's reins to what I took to be the pointed stump of a tree. I lay down and slept.

I dreamt that I was back in the tropical heat of Ceylon. When I woke up it was daylight. I was astonished to find myself in a village, lying in a churchyard. I heard Never You Mind neighing, but when I looked around he was not to be seen.

Then I looked up. My good horse was hanging by his bridle from the weathercock on the church's steeple.

I understood at once. When I arrived the village had been covered by a snowdrift which reached to the church tower's top. During the night the weather changed for the warmer. The snow had melted.

I had sunk down to the churchyard in my sleep, gently, as the snow melted away. What I thought to be a tree stump was the top of the steeple.

Without thinking twice I took my pistol, shot the bridle in two, caught Never You Mind in my arms, mounted him and rode off in the direction of Russia.

The first Russian I met embraced me.

"Baron Munchausen!" he cried.

"And by whom do I have the honor of being hugged?" I asked.

"Pardon me," he said. "I am the Czar of Russia. They call me Peter the Great."

"I am glad to meet you, Peter," I said.

"Oh, Baron, will you please lead my armies against the Turks?"

"Certainly not," I replied.

But then the poor Czar argued, pleaded and finally begged – so I gave in.

It would be boastful to list the victories which followed. Let Peter the Great take the glory.

But there was an amusing incident when we took Constantinople. I had galloped, on Never You Mind, far ahead of my armies.

The Turkish Army was fleeing before me. I thundered after them through the West Gate of the city and chased them out of the East Gate.

I stopped in the market-place and watched them vanish. But when I looked around I was surprised to see that my armies had still not arrived in the city.

Never You Mind was panting. I rode him to a horse trough and he began to drink. I had never known him to drink so many gallons. But I understood his thirst when I looked behind me.

The hind quarters and back legs of the poor creature were missing. He had been cut in half. The water was running out of him as fast as he could drink it.

How had this happened? I found out when I rode his front half back, very gently, to the West Gate. When we had ridden through the gate, the enemy had dropped the portcullis – a heavy falling iron door with spikes at the bottom. This had cut off Never You Mind's back parts. His belly, buttocks, tail and hind legs were waiting anxiously for me outside the gate. And so were my armies.

This might have been the end of my good horse. But I managed to bring together the front and back halves of Never You Mind while they were still hot.

I sewed them up with young shoots of laurel. These bound Never You Mind together neatly. He was, within hours, as fit as a fireplace.

The laurel sprigs grew and formed a curving, leafy arch over my head when I rode. This proved to be a great benefit in hot countries, where I was protected from the sun by the shade of my laurels.

And how did I travel home to my parents and my 48 sisters and brothers? Never You Mind.

And that's as true as treacle.